T0198800

I Am Awesome!

By Ryan K. Maule

Illustrations by L.M. Phang

WestBow Press books may be ordered through booksellers or by contacting:

WestBow Press
A Division of Thomas Nelson & Zondervan
1663 Liberty Drive
Bloomington, IN 47403
www.westbowpress.com
1 (866) 928-1240

Because of the dynamic nature of the Internet, any web addresses or links contained
in this book may have changed since publication and may no longer be valid. The views
expressed in this work are solely those of the author and do not necessarily reflect the
views of the publisher, and the publisher hereby disclaims any responsibility for them.

Any people depicted in stock imagery provided by Getty Images are models,
and such images are being used for illustrative purposes only.
Certain stock imagery © Getty Images.

Interior Image Credit: L.M. Phang

Scripture quotations are from the ESV® Bible (The Holy Bible, English Standard Version®), copyright © 2001
by Crossway, a publishing ministry of Good News Publishers. Used by permission. All rights reserved.

ISBN: 978-1-9736-8105-2 (sc)
ISBN: 978-1-9736-8128-1 (e)

Library of Congress Control Number: 2019919562

Print information available on the last page.

WestBow Press rev. date: 02/13/2020

So God created man in his own image,
in the image of God he created him;
male and female he created them.

Genesis 1:27

Welcome to the land of good!

Goodland is a beautiful place filled with amazing inventions, both big and small, and everyone here comes together to be good friends, good neighbors, good workers, and good members of the community.

At the heart of Goodland lives the Inventor. The Inventor creates all the things in Goodland. He invents the most beautiful flowers. The tallest trees. The greenest grass. He invents incredible creatures, wonderful foods, and paints the most amazing sunsets at bed time.

Of all the things the inventor has created, the followers are his favorite. The followers live all over Goodland. They are always trying to do good and if you ask a follower how they are doing, they will always tell you that they are good!

One of those followers is named Grace. Grace is a kind purple follower who is very curious, outgoing, and thoughtful. Her best friend's name is Zeal! Zeal may be smaller and shorter than Grace, but he shines as bright as the blue paint on his follower body. He loves to smile, talks a lot, and is very protective of Grace. They are always together - playing, learning, eating, and sharing.

One day, as Grace and Zeal were playing a fun game of chase in the middle of the park, they ran into a new follower fishing by the lake. "Good day," Grace greeted, "What's your name?"

"My name is Hope!"

"Hi Hope, I'm Zeal, and this is my best friend Grace! How are you today?"

"It's good to meet you both! I AM AWESOME!" Hope replied.

"What do you mean, you're awesome?" Grace asked in confusion, "You're not good?"

"I'm better than good! I am awesome!"

This took both Grace and Zeal by surprise. No one had ever said they were awesome before. This was the land of good. Everyone has always just been good. Why would this follower be any different?

"I think you're confused Hope," Grace replied, "The only person in Goodland that we know of that is awesome is the Inventor. Everyone else is good! Don't you mean you're good?"

"No," said Hope, "I'm not just good, I am awesome! In fact, I just left the Inventor's workshop and when I said I was awesome, the Inventor gave me a high five and said 'yes you are.'"

This couldn't be possible. Neither Grace nor Zeal had ever met an awesome follower before. How can this be?

After saying goodbye to Hope, Grace and Zeal needed answers.

"We need to get to the bottom of this," said Grace.

"Yeah," replied Zeal, "let's go talk to the Inventor and get the truth!"

As fast as they could, Grace and Zeal ran down the straight and narrow path to the Inventor's workshop. Luckily, the Inventor's doors are always open both day and night and everyone is welcome to come in. No matter how busy or the time of day, the Inventor always has time to stop and talk to the followers.

"Come in Grace and Zeal," the Inventor called while working on a new creation, "what can I do for two of my favorite inventions?"

"Well sir," Grace began, "we were playing in the park when we ran into a new follower named Hope who claimed to be awesome and not good!"

"Yeah!" Zeal added, "Can you believe it?! We thought you needed to know so you could set the record straight!"

"HmmHmmHmm," the Inventor chuckled before composing himself. "Thank you both for bringing this to my attention. I can definitely clear this up. But first let me ask you a few questions about your definition of awesome.

Do you think the trees and the grass that I invented in Goodland are awesome?"

"Of course!" Zeal chimed.

"What about all the foods I invented, the flowers that fill the park, the purple and pink sunsets? I've invented a lot of things. Are all those things awesome?"

"Yes! Yes! Those things are awesome too!" replied Grace. "And what about me? Do you think that I am awesome?"

Both Grace and Zeal nodded their heads in agreement, "You ARE awesome!"

"Well then," the Inventor responded, "If I am awesome, and everything I invent is awesome, doesn't that make you awesome since I invented you?"

"Wait, what?" Asked Zeal.

"When I invented you, I wanted to create something that could represent me to everyone and all things. I wanted you to be a reflection of all that I am. Everything you admire about me, is in you. Everything that you love about me is in you. Everything that is awesome about me is in you. You were created in my own image. My awesomeness is your awesomeness!"

"But we live in Goodland?! Doesn't that make us good?" Grace asked nervously.

"Yes Grace, you are good. You, Zeal, Hope, and all the other inventions in Goodland are good. But you're also so much more than that. You are awesome! You can do awesome things! You have the ability to take the awesome inside of you and multiply it throughout Goodland!

You see, I created Goodland as a place for you to do more. I didn't plant you in the ground like a tree. I didn't stick you in the sky like a star. I didn't make you to be walked on like the grass. You were made to do awesome things! You were created with an awesome purpose and I gave you that purpose for one simple reason. You and all the other followers are my greatest invention! And as my greatest invention, I expect way more from you than all the other things in Goodland. I expect awesome from you."

"So, you're saying that I am awesome?" Zeal asked.

"Yes Zeal, that's exactly what I'm saying," replied the Inventor. "Let's try it out! Zeal, how are you?"

"I am awesome!" Zeal responded.

"What about you Grace? How are you?"

"I am awesome!"

"Yes, you are." With a giggle and a smile, the Inventor lifted his hand and gave each a high five before telling them proudly, "You. Are. Awesome."

ABOUT THE AUTHOR:

Ryan K. Maule

Ryan is a nationally recognized and highly sought-after motivational speaker, host of the popular Expect Awesome Podcast, and the president of Integrity Doctors, the world's largest chiropractic business organization. Over the last 15 years Ryan has traveled the world spreading the message of expecting awesome and building a stronger self-image in order to gain a God powered confidence. Ryan is happily married to his awesome wife Amber and they live in Florida with their two awesome kids, Summer Grace and Nolan Zeal. For more information visit ryankmaule.com

Printed in the United States
By Bookmasters